Rabén & Sjögren Bokförlag, Stockholm
www.raben.se

Originally published in Sweden by Rabén & Sjögren under the title
Nöff nöff Benny

Library of Congress Control Number: 2007930332
Printed in Denmark
First American edition, 2008

ISBN-13: 978-91-29-66855-1
ISBN-10: 91-29-66855-7

Barbro Lindgren · Olof Landström

Oink, Oink Benny

Translated by
Elisabeth Kallick Dyssegaard

Stockholm New York London Adelaide Toronto

Benny is going out. He's tired of hanging around inside.

Benny's little brother is also tired of hanging around inside.
They are going to go out and have some fun.

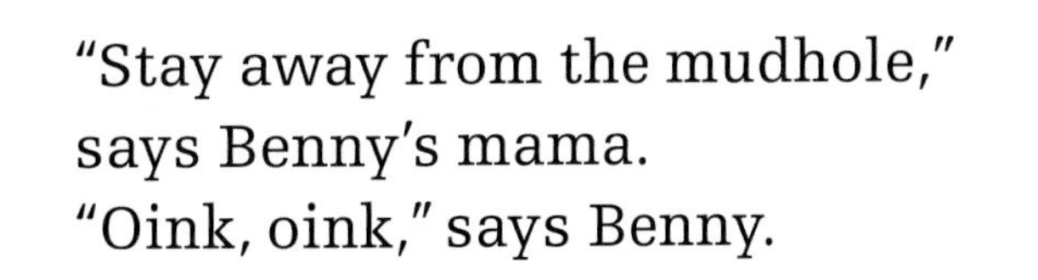

"Stay away from the mudhole,"
says Benny's mama.
"Oink, oink," says Benny.

First they goof off for a bit.

Then they head straight for the mudhole.

Everyone is there. Some of their friends are really dumb. Some are really nice. Klara is the nicest.

Benny loves Klara. His little brother loves Klara, too.
"Do you want to run around the mudhole?" asks Klara.
"Oink," says Benny.
"Oink, oink," says his little brother.

Then they run.

It's fun to run around the mudhole. They run faster and faster.

But then mean old Rafe sneaks up.

SPLASH! He pushes Benny's little brother into the mudhole.

Benny's little brother screams for his life.
Then Klara jumps in and saves him!

Later, he gets to sit on her knee with his snout against her cheek. Benny's little brother is very happy. But Benny is very sad. He also wants to sit on Klara's knee with his snout against her cheek.

That's why he falls into the mudhole, too.

Klara saves him as well!
He also gets to sit on Klara's knee
with his snout against her cheek.

After a while, Benny gets tired of sitting on Klara's knee.
His little brother also gets tired of sitting on Klara's knee.
Now they want to go home and hang out there instead.

But they are very dirty and very wet. Their mama is going to be able to see right away that they have been to the mudhole and fallen in. What are they going to do now?
"We can hide in the forest," says Benny.
"Yes, we can hide in the forest," says his little brother.

They hide under a big pine tree.

But it is much too dark under the pine. They have to find another place to hide. It's too dark everywhere though. And there are no lights in the forest.

“We’ll run home,” says Benny.
“Oink,” says his little brother.
And then they run home.

Suddenly it starts to rain. Now they get even wetter than before!

“Oh, poor children, look how wet you are,” says their mama.
“Come in so I can dry you off.”

Now Benny wants to be inside. He's tired of
goofing off outside.
His little brother is also tired of goofing off outside.
They'll never go out again.

(But the next day, they go out anyway!)